T0197576

Hilary and Belle

Reva VanNoy Smith

Illustrated by
Valerie Brooks Plaisance

Copyright © 2022 by Reva Van Nay Smith. 833709

All rights reserved. No part of this book may
be reproduced or transmitted in any form or by
any means, electronic or mechanical, including
photocopying, recording, or by any information storage
and retrieval system, without permission in writing from
the copyright owner.

This is a work of fiction. Names, characters,
places and incidents either are the product of the
author's imagination or are used fictitiously, and any
resemblance to any actual persons, living or dead,
events, or locales is entirely coincidental.

To order additional copies of this book, contact:
Xlibris
844-714-8691
www.Xlibris.com
Orders@Xlibris.com

ISBN: 978-1-6698-4308-5 (sc)
ISBN: 978-1-6698-4307-8 (e)

Print information available on the last page

Rev. date: 09/14/2022

This journey would not have been possible without the support and encouragement
of many whom I'd like to acknowledge and thank.

First and foremost is my loving family —
my husband Lonnie, plus our children, Ashley, Lonnie Jr., and Shae.
My husband boosted my confidence and cheered me on throughout this entire process.
That kept me on point and excited about each page and the deep message of the book.

I would like to thank Carolyn Henry, my dear friend since 7th grade who has read everything
that I've ever written over the last twenty plus years. The Novel is coming!

I must extend my deepest gratitude to my Illustrator and cousin, Valerie Plaisance.
Her input, expertise, and professionalism far exceeded any expectations I had of what an Illustrator may bring to
the table. Her knowledge of this process helped me get to this point. Her artwork went above and beyond the
simplistic characters I had imagined for this book, and I am grateful.

I dedicate this first book to my precious grandchildren, Pierce and Mariah.
To them, I say, "May you aim high, never quit, and always follow your dreams."

Reva

This is in loving memory of my devoted parents, Edwin Brooks and Forrestine VanNoy Brooks,
who gave me my first dog, a Skye Terrier named Hey Boy, my art tools (pencil, pen, paintbrush),
and encouraged me to always strive for excellence.

With a heart full of gratitude,
I thank my daughter Michelle, my loudest cheerleader,
who continued to love me even though I spent hundreds of hours
drawing and painting in my studio,
when we could have been out galivanting together.

It was a tremendous honor to collaborate with the author.
Working (virtually) alongside Reva on this thrilling journey with Hilary and Belle
from concept to book has been unlike any other venture I've experienced.
What a ride! I'm ready for another.

Valerie

Hilary and Belle

Reva VanNoy Smith

Illustrated by
Valerie Brooks Plaisance

When they told me
you were coming

I must admit

I was afraid

When they said you were from
a Shelter

I wondered how long you had
Stayed

I WONDERED IF YOU'D BE
HAPPY IN YOUR NEW HOME

WITH A SISTER YOU'D NEVER MET
I WONDERED IF YOU'D HAD YOUR SHOTS

OR EVEN BEEN TO THE VET?

YOU SEE THEY SAY THAT
I'M A PRINCESS
AND I'M USED TO THINGS A
CERTAIN WAY.

SO I WONDERED IF YOU'D
BE OKAY WITH THAT

AND YEAH I WONDERED IF YOU'D STAY.

THEY SAY YOU'RE A RESCUED
BOXER
AND LOVED BY ALL YOU MEET.

YOU SEE, I AM A PIT BULL
AND SO
MANY ARE AFRAID OF ME

I'M NOT SURE WHY PEOPLE
SEE US DIFFERENTLY

WE WAG OUR TAILS THE VERY SAME WAY.

WE BOTH LIKE TO RUN AND SNIFF
ROLLOVER AND BARK

AND PLAY
ALL THROUGH THE DAY

WELL ACTUALLY WHEN I
THINK ABOUT IT
THAT LAST SENTENCE
ISN'T TRUE

I'D REALLY RATHER LAY
AROUND AND SLEEP ALL DAY

HA HA HOW ABOUT YOU?

I GUESS I'LL FIND OUT
SOON ENOUGH
BECAUSE TODAY IS THE DAY
WE MEET

I'M SURE YOU WILL WANT TO
LAY IN MY BED

I'M SURE YOU WILL WANT MY
TREATS!

I'M STARTING TO GET
NERVOUS
AS YOU COME RUNNING
THROUGH THE DOOR

YOU QUICKLY RUN HERE,
AND RUN QUICKLY THERE,

YOU'RE ALL OVER THE FLOOR

I'M NOT SURE
I EVEN WANT YOU HERE

FOR A DAY

FOR A MONTH

AND SURELY NOT A YEAR

I MUST SAY YOU'RE PRETTY PLAYFUL

WE MIGHT GET ALONG AFTER ALL

AS LONG AS YOU STAY AWAY FROM
MY BED, MY TREATS
AND MY BALL!

MY MOMMY SAYS LET'S GO
OUTSIDE

I GUESS SHE'S NOW YOUR
MOMMY TOO

HOW EVER DO YOU RUN SO FAST?

I CAN'T KEEP UP WITH YOU!

I GUESS THE SHELTER
WAS NOT THAT BAD AFTER ALL

YOU SEEM HAPPY AS CAN BE

AND MUCH TO MY SURPRISE
YOU BOUGHT
YOUR OWN TOYS I SEE.

THE FACT THAT I'M A PRINCESS
PIT BULL
DOES NOT SEEM TO BOTHER YOU

YOU DON'T SEEM TO HAVE
CARE IN THE WORLD
WE'RE GOING TO HAVE
SO MUCH FUN!

WOO HOO!!

ALL THE DAYS I SPENT AFRAID
I SHOULD HAVE LISTENED
TO MY MOM AND DAD

THEY TOLD ME ONCE
THEY TOLD ME TWICE

YOU'RE GOING TO LOVE HILARY
AND YOU'LL BE GLAD

BELLE AND HILARY
HILARY AND BELLE

WHAT WILL WE DO NEXT?
ONLY TIME WILL TELL

THE END

Reva VanNoy Smith

has been writing short stories, lyrics, and poetry for more than twenty years. The adventures of Hilary and Belle is her first venture into writing children's books. While growing up in Kansas City, Missouri, Reva always dreamed of someday becoming a veterinarian. Much to her surprise, after working at a vet clinic, she quickly realized that operating on dogs and loving them were two different things. And this instantly changed her career path. Reva's abiding love and deep passion for both animals and fine literature converged, inspired by Hilary and Belle, two beloved family pets. This is book number one of a heartwarming trilogy that teaches young readers how important and easy it is to accept others who may not have the same background or look alike, because we're all identical on the inside. Everyone wants to feel safe, happy, and loved. As Hilary says in the book, all dogs like to run, sniff, rollover, bark, play, and wag their tails the very same way. This book teaches us that our many remarkable commonalities outnumber our differences.

Valerie Brooks Plaisance

is a mixed media artist, working with acrylic paint, permanent ink, pastel chalk, crayon, and more. She can usually be found in her studio, filled with canvases, paints & brushes galore, finished pieces on the walls, and works in progress on easels. If not in her studio, she's out running in preparation for her next 5k race or reading or crocheting or teaching an art class or having raucous fun with her family and Winston the giant schnauzer. Valerie's very first "studio" was her childhood back porch. At age 7, she deemed herself an artist when her parents gave her a No.2 pencil, a ballpoint pen, and a paintbrush. Those precious tools fit nicely in an empty cigar box, along with the discarded 2" by 3" cookie cards she collected from her friends' lunchboxes, cleverly repurposed as "canvases." Her "paint" was water in a cup and her "masterpieces" were short-lived images on the porch cement. Time passed and she chose a teaching career to pair with Artist. Inspired by Vincent van Gogh, Valerie studied his life extensively, and used his works of art across the curriculum, creating a direct connection to Math, Science, Social Studies, and so forth. Validation came when she received the prestigious BRAVO Award for her unconventional teaching style and demonstrating excellence in art education. So it's no surprise that this book is full of van Gogh connections, too!

Printed in the United States
by Baker & Taylor Publisher Services